Bloody Battle

Bloody Battle

ALDIVAN TORRES

Canary Of Joy

Contents

{ 1 }

"Bloody Battle"
Aldivan Torres
Bloody Battle

Author: Aldivan Torres
© 2020- Aldivan Torres
All rights reserved

This book, including all parts, is copyrighted and may not be reproduced without the permission of the author, resold or downloaded.

Aldivan Torres is a psychologist, doctor and screenwriter. A fan of literature and science fiction, he intends to revolutionize literature. Literary fame is not everything, what matters is the message.

2.76-Justiciers again in action

Back to the question of battles between the two sides, each instant the two groups were stronger in the development of the powers of their integral. While the evil side had a pentagon amulet as a weapon the good ones trained with their worldly crucifix chains.

Knowing you were outnumbered, Angel, you only intended a new action when you were sure of a good response from your commanders. This happened a month after the last fight. She was called a rush meeting with the remaining members of the vigilante group to perform at the usual place.

On the day, schedule and location, everyone actually showed up the ones who lived far away. Gently, they were answered by the host at the door and forwarded to a place reserved inside the house. With everyone well settled, the exits were locked and immediately the meeting was initiated.

Angel, as chief, was the first to take the word:

"Well, my dear fellows, I called you here because we have to resolve the matter of the land invasion by the Colonel. The owners can't stand at the mercy of this corrupt.

"I agree. But how can we overcome the opponent's barrier? (VICTOR)

"The answer is inside yourselves. I gave each of you the most powerful symbol in the universe helped by him, in a joint force, we can again triumph. (Angel)

"Okay. What about the risks? (Penelope)

"There'll always be my face. But I believe in your potential. (I said it with confidence Angel)

"I'm with you, master. I'm sure my love, wherever you are, would approve my attitude. (Marcela)

"Thank you, Marcela. You can be sure Roman's blood was not in vain. (Angel)

"So, what are we waiting for? Come on (Rafael)

"Yes. This time we're going to maximum power. Everyone's climbing. Put your masks on and leave as soon as possible! (Ordered Angel)

"With me. One for all and one for all! (VICTOR)

Everyone came close, they held hands, and they repeated the phrase of Victor in choir. After they split up, they took the masks and settled the last details before they left. With everything ready, they finally left headquarters and headed for the main site of the conflict. Forward, vigilantes, we're with you!

Soon as they first came, they turned so no one would notice their presences. They were only detected when they were very close to their opponents, and it was at this point that a new embassy began.

Bloody Battle

This one was all against everyone, randomly. As they were already on their well-developed techniques, the dispute was equal to equal, with amazing effects. For 30 minutes, there was no death. There were only some slight injuries.

As nothing decided, each began to use its backup and mystical strength. In this last part, the vigilantes took advantage of strength and faith. With this, the opponents were falling one by one. Completely overdue, asked for mercy, and were thrown out of the scene.

The land then occupied were released for use of the rightful. After receiving the thanks, they began the return to the location of origin. As close as it was, they quickly arrived. They gave the master the good news, celebrate the accomplishment and made the plan for the next steps of the group.

In the end, they were released because each had to do their job. Another victory for good in this hard battle! Keep it that way.

2.77- The Secrets of Levitation

Excited by one more victory of your group, Victor, and his wife have returned to their routine activities. Between work, social activities, leisure, and teamwork filled out their time until Sunday arrival. This moment when it was completed approximately a month of the last healer's meeting.

Full of will and disposition, the disciple departed immediately to meet the master after he's settled some pertinent details. Here in 15 minutes of fast walk, passing through vegetation and relief once known, the same has finally arrived at the humble Healer's hovel. This was the inmate of the domain techniques of good and evil.

In front of the little house, the disciple for a little frozen by a sudden fear. But this moment doesn't last long because soon after it moves and keeps moving forward. Then you come by the door and knock on the door.

In moments, from within, the mysterious known figure of the master. After greeting him, he leads him to what in the house represented the room. It's in this room where the grass bed was located and an old trunk.

They sit on the bed, the looks cross, anticipate great revelations. As always, the healer takes the initiative:

"How have you been?

"Very well Our group has achieved important victories and every day I learn a little more. What do we get for today? (VICTOR)

"I'll teach you the levitation technique. It'll be very helpful. (Healer)

"How? Can I fly already? (IMAGINED THE DISCREDIT VICTOR)

"They're separate things. I'll teach you not only the levitation of the body, but also the levitation of the spirit. Whoever dominates it is capable of, in case you concentrate enough, penetrate other worlds. However, this miracle is something that you reach only with a lot of effort, persistence, and experience. That's not your case for now. (Healer)

"Got it Then teach me. (VICTOR)

"Very well. Lie normally in bed, looking at the ceiling. (Healer)

The servant obeyed the master's command. When he got really comfortable, he asked impatient:

"What now? What's the next step?

"First, release your inner mind, fixing your thought to the far point your imagination reaches. When you reach this point, pronounce this secret word: Inkirin! From there, you'll be able to break the chains that prevent you from having control over your body and the force of gravity. Ready? (Healer)

"I'll try. (VICTOR)

Even without understanding the depth of the Shaman's words, the apprentice began the attempt phase: tried once, two, three times unsuccessfully. Finally, on Wednesday, oriented again, succeeded.

Wonderful with the technique, spent more than two hours practicing it until it exhausted its physical possibilities. That's when the healer intervened again:

"Easy, Victor, you don't have to overreact. You can go if you want.

"You're right. Thank you for everything, master. One day, I'll make it up to you. (VICTOR)

"Don't worry. See you in about a month, same Sunday as usual? (healer)

"Yeah, sure. You can count it. See you later. (VICTOR)

"See you later. (Healer)

Victor is going to the exit. With a few steps, he walked past the door and finally reached the outside. Following the usual path, began the short course back. When I got home, I'd sort out some loose ends, take care of the woman, get some rest, meditate a little and make some plans for the future. Every step he took, he was getting closer to the truth and then fate was preparing for him. Let's move on.

2.78-Visitor and posterior experience

Exactly the day after a recent meeting with the healer, during work break time, Victor will meet a scream and a strong knock on the door of his residence. When you open the door, you find nothing more than your dear brother Rafael, battle mate. After a hug and kissing on the fancy face, both come into the house, heading into the room. Once you get to the room, you settle in chairs, one across the other. The conversation is then initiated:

"What a surprise, brother. What are you doing here? (VICTOR)

"I came for two reasons. First, to kill the missed you and bring back memories of our mother. Second to ask for advice. (Rafael)

"Thank you. But what can I do for you? (VICTOR)

"Like I said, I want some advice You know, brother, I'm no boy anymore, and every day you pass I feel lonely. What do I do? (Rafael)

"If I understand correctly, you're passing sexual deprivation. Is that it? (VICTOR)

"Yes. But don't spread it. (Rafael's restrained laugh)

"Well, in my case, I had experience with trusted people, and it didn't take long to get married. Today I'm satisfied. (VICTOR)

"What do you advise me then? (Rafael)

"Well, if you want, I can take you to a cabaret. I think it's the best way out (VICTOR)

"Cabaret? How does it work? (Rafael)

"It's an environment with prostitutes. You come in, have a drink, and when you grow up, you call one of the girls. Just like that. (VICTOR)

"Perfect. Shall we go then? (Rafael)

"Just wait a minute, I'll talk to my wife. (VICTOR)

Victor goes to the kitchen and there goes with his wife some details (explains to go out with his brother and asks for the same replacement in the market). After all is settled, he returns to the place where his brother is found.

Both of you finally leave They're past the exit door, they're taking the main street, and with five minutes of fast walk, they're coming to the brothel. Victor stops at this instant, he passes his brother's last guidance, gives him money and leaves to avoid the bad languages.

Nearly the entrance, alone, Rafael was meeting. Now it was him, the courage and the destiny that were about to reveal itself. What would happen?

Driven by instinct curiosity and need Rafael finally decide to enter after a few moments of quick reflection. One, two, three, ten steps and you're already in the salon of the bar that was attached to a few rooms.

He approaches a table, sits and checks the presence of several men, of all the age lanes and attractive women, stripped, impudent. One of them gives signal to the same and approaches.

At your approach, Rafael feels his spine cold. What now? How do you act? The blonde girl with the nice faces and the good wingspan, looking at about five years longer than the same, sits next to her and embraces her waist. This attitude only increases the boy's nerves and the girl, experienced, realizes his innocence and tries to make an approach.

"Hi, my name is Claudia and you?

"Rafael. (STAMMERING)

"Calm down. Would you like something to ease the tension? (Claudia)

"What's to drink? (Rafael)

"I'd recommend you a good drink. But in moderate dose, so you don't lose consciousness. (Claudia)

"Okay. Bring it. (Rafael)

Claudia steps away for a moment. He goes to the shelf, he picks the drink, opens the same, and fills a glass in half. Thereafter, he returns to the table where Rafael is found. When you arrive, you deliver the drink immediately. Retake the dialogue.

"It's here. Take it slow.

Rafael, with the glass in his hand, he takes it towards the mouth and when he touches it, he starts pouring on the same liquid. As it was your first time, strange a little flavor and finish by giving up the rest.

Immediately, there's a reaction in his system that makes him more cheerful, free, loose and fearless. Taking the initiative, he takes Claudia by the waist and invites her to a contradiction because a song starts to be played. She accepts.

Both are heading to the center of the hall. Directed by a strange force begin to understand each other completely. They exchange caresses, conversations, and in the end, it ends with a sugary kiss on the mouth.

Immediately, Claudia invites you to get to know each other better in a room. With the strength of the drink, Rafael gets carried away. Together, the two of you move away from the others, turn right, and enter room number three.

Close the door and both help each other undress. When they're completely naked, Claudia takes him to bed. The same teaches the apprentice every step of love well done, foreplay, the boldest caresses, oral sex, anal and vaginal in every possible position until it gets to the ultimate ecstasy, the full orgasm, multiple orgasm.

After they rest and sleep. Three hours later, they wake up. Rafael says thanks and pays the bill. She says goodbye without commitments and no date of right return because she won't return until she feels too much need.

Heads the exit. When you reach the street, you feel better and at the same time. Casual sex was good, but it didn't fill the void that I felt inside my chest, the loneliness of day to day. I hoped in faith that you would find true love, a strong reason to live. He deserved to be happy because he was always a good person.

Rafael comes to his brother's house. He just comes in to say goodbye to him and his wife. Have a sip of water and you're leaving. The long journey is begun to the back Situation.

They would only see each other at the meeting of the group that were participating or at any other time that they were unoccupied. Although distant, the same conserved the same friendship as always and that was rare because usually brothers were rivals.

They were the famous Torres. They were ready to make their mark in history for their bravery, dignity, loyalty, and values. Forever, Punishers!

2.79-A visit from Sara.

The rest of the week went without any big news. The work rhythm at the market was still intense, the integral of both opposite sides continued to perfection their powers and the colonel was still influential. Nothing was decided at all.

In the entrance of the new week, two events: Joseph Pereira's judgment and with evidence gathered, sentenced to three years of seclu-

Bloody Battle

sion, a sudden urge that filled the senses with Professor Sara to see Victor, to speak to his wife, to speak to his life and his heart. That's how without thinking much too traveled to Carabais.

During the long way, made on the loin of a horse, had the opportunity to reflect, analyze and live a new experience that made her remember her childhood in the Big Bang Place. Those were the days, he was younger, totally innocent, and free to love. At least that's what I thought because traditionally, I had a disappointment.

But this was not the time to blame yourself or mourn. It was time for renewal and hoped that with this new encounter it could finally free your suffering heart, break for another and be happy. She wasn't the only one. Ninety-nine percent of the people who had suffered loving disappointments wished it and were worthy of success and happiness. Like me!

With this intimate will to start over, ends by fulfilling the considerable path in a normal time. Right in the village, it's reported to the location of Victor's residence. When you pick this data, you leave immediately for the site.

As everything in Carabais was close, it doesn't take long and the same is already on the front door of the house screaming and knocking. Immediately, you hear noise from steps that approaches and hopes to be answered.

The door then opens. She has the opportunity once again to contemplate the face and the characteristic paths of his childhood love that appears surprised to see her right there. Victor takes the word:

"What are you doing here?

"I came to visit you and your wife. I want to talk a little and kill the people. Can I come in?

"Sure, at ease. After all, we're not friends anymore.

Both of you go into the house and head to the room. When he reaches the room, Victor offers one of the chairs as a seat. She accepts and settles. After he goes to the kitchen calls his wife and together return to the initial site.

They greet and start talking like adults they are.

"To what do I owe the honor of the visit, Professor? (Penelope)

"I already told your husband. I wanted to talk to you for a while, see you guys because we've been away for a long time. (Sara)

"True. Since we got married, we've been very busy, and we haven't had time to see friends at headquarters. How's school? (Penelope)

"Well, as far as possible, but sad about Ramon's death. He was a great student and a good person. (Sara)

"We're sorry too. He was one of ours.

"How's Marcela? (Sara)

"Well, it seems to have overcome the initial shock of the event. (Penelope)

"But that doesn't mean you won't forget. I mean it from experience. (VICTOR)

"I agree. I also lived through the experience of losing a loved one. (Sara)

"How about you? Did you get a boyfriend yet? (Penelope)

"No, I just had a little flirt, but mine blew it. (CONFESSED SARA)

"What was his name? (Penelope)

"Victor, your current husband. (Sara)

Sara's revelation left Penelope static for a few seconds. I never suspected that the two of you had such a close connection. When he recovered from the shock, he resumed the conversation.

"Why didn't you tell me? Betrayed is the last to know, isn't it? (Penelope)

"Wait a minute. I never betrayed you. My affair with Sara was before I met you when I was a kid. (VICTOR)

"True. There's been nothing between us since. Don't suspect your husband. (Sara)

"Okay. But don't get your hopes up because you're already committed. (PENELOPE)

"I know. Don't worry. I know how to respect other people's men. (Sara)

Bloody Battle

"I would never betray you. We'd talk first. But that's not the case. (VICTOR)

"Well, what I meant to say is that I wish all the happiness in the world for you. My goal here is to overcome the past once and for all and start a new life. I'm free to meet someone. (Sara)

"Good. You're right. Find happiness, and you'll find it at some point. (Penelope)

"Yes, everyone deserves to be happy. Despite what we live, we can be friends, right? (VICTOR)

"Sure, friends, after all. Give me a hug. (Sara)

All three of them got up from the chairs. When they met, there was a triple hug, wrapped in a lot of emotion. Finally, things were clearing up and taking their place. I'll give her a hug, Sara's pronounced herself again.

"Well, that was all. I'm going to go. Thank you for your attention.

"Calm down. Don't you want something to eat? (Offered gently Penelope)

"I'll have some water. (Sara)

"I'll get it. (Penelope)

Five minutes is the time Penelope takes to fulfill the request and return to the room. Deliver the glass with the liquid and the visitor takes it quickly. Then he finally says goodbye to both of you, heading towards the exit. It crosses the obstacle and, out, rides the horse starting the long way back quieter.

When I got home, it would be a new Sara. Ready to love and be loved. Far away from the ghosts of the past. Keep following, readers.

2.80-Ambush

With defeat in the last battle, the evil representatives were engaged to recover, divided between training and planning. In a sequence of meetings, they ended up having a magnificent idea of expelling the vigilantes.

First, rumors were spreading in the village that they would have kidnapped helpless children. The second step was to be staked waiting for the opponents to target them surprised.

Coming to the ears of the vigilantes, naively was organized a counteroffensive composed by three members, Rafael, Victor, and Marcela. The three, munitions of the sense of justice, quickly headed towards Carabais farm headquarters where the children were supposed to be.

After a while of walking, approximately halfway, they were intercepted by the evil mutants and then began another battle.

Even with the numerical advantage to the maleficent team, the embassy presented itself balanced from beginning to end, in a total of thirty minutes of exercise.

At the end of this time, feeling exhausted, the fight was over. The bosses of the groups gathered and combined a final fight to perform at the most in a month when the winning group would finally know. After the meeting, everyone went back to their respective homes. What now? What would happen?

Whatever the result, everyone was congratulating on the respective dedication to the cause whether it's fair or not. Let's move on.

2.8٫-learnt double

Time goes on and on. It arrives exactly on the day scheduled for the sixth learning meeting between the Healer and his disciple Victor. From early on, the last one prepared for this meeting that promised to be revealing and quite interesting just as the previous ones were.

When he was completely ready, Victor says goodbye to his wife and finally leaves towards the goal concluding this short course in the predicted time. It approaches the hovel and as the door was open, it takes the liberty to enter unexpected because it was already considered home.

As you enter the room, you find the master sitting on the floor, in a position of meditation, with eyes closed and appearing to be very focused. With a little fear, he takes the liberty of coming along and with a touch tries to wake him up. The strategy has effect because immediately the healer rises and then the dialogue is initiated.

"Glad you're here. I have something important to transmit. (Healer)

"What? Something serious? (VICTOR)

"Serious. The pact you made shortened time. This will be our last encounter of perfection. But you will not be harmed. I'll teach you double today. (Healer)

"Got it. What will you teach me today? (VICTOR)

"I'll teach you to play fate, have a domain of free will and above all else have the courage for what's coming. Are you ready? (Healer)

"Well, I guess so. You can start. (VICTOR)

With the disciple's positive response, the master has gone for a moment. He went to his room. When I returned, I brought with you a crystal ball. With a signal, he asked the disciple to sit down and do that he gave him the ball. From this moment on, he began to give you instructions.

"Fix the eye on the ball by giving back memories, present and possible future. What do you see?

"In the past, I see fights, misunderstandings, suffering. As for the present, a broken situation between successes and failures. However, the future presents itself completely blurry. What does it mean? (VICTOR)

"It means that your future and those around you will depend on your free will. It's going to be a very difficult decision to make. (Healer)

"What do you advise me? (VICTOR)

"Follow your common sense and your heart. Remember the cause. I also want to say that I will support you in your decision and I will be present, helping in this final battle. Do you want some? (Healer)

"Are you confident? I don't know what ratios this dispute will come. (VICTOR)

"I don't care. I've made a mistake in this life and I want to hit you, supporting you, the vigilantes, against evil and elites! We're together! (healer)

The statement of support of the current master has thrilled Victor. Both hugged at a time of quite complicity. One for all and one for all! From this moment on, the healer was also integrated with the group and whatever God wanted.

At the end of the hug, they moved a little away and the dialogue was rebooted.

"Okay. In a week it'll be the battle. We'll meet at Angel's house at eight o'clock in the morning, and then we'll leave. (VICTOR)

"Deal. I'll be there. I hope the others don't mind. (Healer)

"Don't worry. Everyone's good. Thank you. Anything else? (VICTOR)

"No. Not for now. See you soon. See you later. (Healer)

"See you later. (VICTOR)

The disciple has moved away and forwarded the exit. You've overstepped the obstacle by having access to the outside. At the same time, I walked through the whole situation that was presented. However, it didn't come to a consensus.

I would follow the master's advice and always listen to the desires of his heart and intuition and see what it was going to do. I'd have enough time for that during the week.

Coming home, relaxed a little and enjoyed the day with the woman. At the end of the day, I'd rest a little more. Until the next chapter.

2.82- The idea.

Since the definitive battle had been set between the two rival groups already known, all the attentions and efforts of the characters involved were bound back to the obtaining victory at any cost.

Bloody Battle

Under that, Angel has set up a secret lightning encounter to perform at your house. Three days from the fight and counting only on the participation of the founding members, him, Victor and Rafael.

The main goal was to gather ideas capable of making them triumph in front of the powerful demand of the elites.

As they were responsible, Victor and Rafael arrived at the date, local and schedule combined dresses in simple and rude suits. They were worldly of a great will to cooperate. They were received by the host at the door with simplicity, humility, and kindness of ever that were their principal features.

After the usual compliments, the three of them went to a corner of the house on the right side. There were already in drum circles in one not so comfortable number. But they were used to worse things.

They settled in the respective seats by exchanging glances of complicity and sympathy. A disturbing silence sets in for a few moments. The spell is broken soon after the steady and grave speech of the Master of Angel Masters:

"Glad you could make it. Friends, the crucial moment has come since we founded the group, our goals, and projects will be at stake and finally find out what fate has in store for us. Any suggestions?

"I have many ideas. I'm thinking of using magic versus magic, light versus dark and involving both sides completely. It might work. What do you think, master? (VICTOR)

"It's a possibility. If things get too hard, do what you think is best. We trust you. (Angel)

"That's it, brother. Among everyone, you are the most prepared because you know both forces. (Observed Rafael)

"Thank you. You're admirable too. How do you act? Have you thought about that? (VICTOR)

"Follow what I taught you: Precaution, strength, and faith at all times. Besides, the union is also necessary because we have monstrous enemies to face. (Angel)

"True. I want to help in the best way I can. (Rafael)

"Me too. Need help, just scream. (VICTOR)

"Well, I've been thinking, how about we call for backup? They'll be needed because we're outnumbered. (Suggested Angel)

"Exactly who did you think of? (VICTOR)

"What do you think of the cangaceiros? They're skilled fighters, they have good guns, contacts, and a lot of race. That would be a big help. (Angel)

"Are you confident? Aren't there many from us? (VICTOR)

"It might be, brother. But at least they're not against us. (Rafael's positioned)

"We have a common goal, fighting the elites. (Angel)

"I support it! (Rafael)

"Well, if you think you're the best, support too. (VICTOR)

"Perfect. I'll take care of the details with a contact I have. We'll meet you in a safe place at the Big Band Place. Agreed? (Angel)

"Yes. (VICTOR AND RAFAEL)

"Well, that's all. You're clear for today. Just do me a favor, call the rest in two days, at this same time at my parents' house. Understood? (Angel)

"Understood, master. (VICTOR CONFIRMED)

"At your service. (Rafael)

"See you later. (Angel)

"See you later. (VICTOR AND RAFAEL)

After the farewell, the two brothers are headed for the exit. In a matter of moments, they're already outside. We each take our course. What would happen? Keep following the next chapters.

2.83- The Cangaceiros

As agreed, Angel contacted one of your acquaintances, a messenger of the lamp pack named Tobias. He explained the situation, handed a note to the chief of the pack and requested urgency in the analysis of the matter. After he came home and then one day, he got the answer.

Bloody Battle

Luckily, it was positive, and it made him vibrate. The current chances of victory became considerable.

He reported the results to the rest of the group, handled his duties by preparing the last details of the trip and the meeting. Everything would have to be perfect. At the end of the day, I was tired, nervous, and distressed by not knowing what was coming. That's why, right after dinner, he took care of sleeping. The other day I promised!

Right after a very troubled evening, it arrived at dawn, normally dawn in the country and in the city. Since early on, the characters in question in their different places have been prepared for events marked to perform in the Fundão Site full of anxiety and nervousness. But this was expected.

When they were ready, they left. For some of them, it would be a long journey. About others, not so much. The important thing was that everyone was getting there in time to talk a bit and settle some more stuff.

Counting on a little dedication, persistence, and luck is what happened. From eight o'clock, the first people were coming in and by nine o'clock, everyone already there. They've gathered as usual in the Magellan family residence room. In addition to the presence of the vigilantes, they also counted on the presence of the hosts.

Angel, as chief, took the initiative to start the conversation:

"Well, my dear friends, I have something to tell you. First, I appreciate the presence and disposition of everyone. (Angel)

"You're welcome. The responsibility is also ours.

"We've been in the same boat since we joined to form this group. (Rafael)

"We thank you for your confidence. (Penelope)

"I'm proud to be part of this team. (Marcela)

"Our son has good news for you. (Maria of conception)

"This. Speak, son. (Geraldo)

"Okay. I've closed a deal with the cangaceiros. They're waiting for us in the woods, heading south. Shall we?

"Fine with me. Come on, guys. (VICTOR)

"Yes. (The rest)

Immediately after the positive response, the visitors fired Angel's parents. Together they're headed to the exit. As they pass the door, they go south, they're shutting down in the woods.

There was a short trajectory to the arranged location of the meeting with the presence of the entire team. Would it work? No one knew and this doubt was the fuel, so everyone could move on without thinking twice about the risks they were taking.

In the process of analyzing the case, they had no choice because the opposing group has been so strong in the last few days, they required special attention from them. The luck was cast.

With steady and regular steps, for twenty-five minutes, that was long enough for them to have access to the south side. It was a place with extensive rocky plains and surrounded by the natural vegetation of aggressive caatinga.

At the sign of the shaman, they stopped. As nothing had happened, the questions before hidden exploded:

"What now? What do we do? (Marcela)

"Easy, girl. I'm sure there's an explanation. (Penelope)

"There always is. (Angel)

"What is it then? (Rafael)

"Calm down. Let the master speak. (VICTOR)

Now, before Angel could answer, from above the trees, they descended one to one of the soldiers of the lamp pack with their typical combat dress. In front of the group, Tobias is approaching.

Getting closer, he tried to explain:

"We're ready. I and these soldiers will help you to overthrow the injustice at once by the elites. Down with coronelism!

"So be it. Why didn't Virgulino come? (Angel)

"As you know, he's a very busy man. He and a part of the pack were to sort out some of the Ceará's stuff. But it is supportive of your cause and so you sent us. (Tobias)

Bloody Battle

"Thank you for all of us. What can we do for you? (VICTOR)

"We want food and accommodations. Only then will we be prepared for tomorrow's combat. (Tobias)

"Sure. You can stay at my house until the time of combat. The others are invited too. (Angel)

"Thank you. Can I stay at your mother's, love? (Penelope)

"You can and you must. You, me, Rafael and Marcela will stay. (VICTOR)

"I do. (Marcela)

"Then it's right like this. Let's go home then. We plan every step because it's important. Let's practice and rest, and tomorrow's another day. (Angel)

"For right and fair! (VICTOR)

"Against the injustices! (Rafael)

"For the weak and indigent! (Penelope)

"For all! (Marcela)

"Cangaceiros and vigilantes, together! (Tobias)

On the signal, everyone greeted themselves by initiating the return to the initial point. They'd come home. They would follow the advice of the respective bosses and at the end of the day they would rest. Furthermore, they couldn't wait for the unrolling of events and the ultimate battle that would decide the fate of all. Let's move on.

2.84-O the other day and the battle.

It's finally dawn. Soon early, the characters in question rise, bathe, eat breakfast and settle the last details before the battle. Specifically, the good group, led by Angel, gather quickly in their home. When they solve all the pending, they're already set for the final card to perform at Colonel Soares' farm, known as Carabais Farm. This meeting promised, for it would come true in the enemy field.

Outside the residence, vigilantes and cangaceiros become invisible. They start to fly, when those who didn't stop this technique are helped by the others. With this, long distance to be traveled would be fulfilled in a minimum time.

During this time, breaking the currents of the air, the group overflows all the exuberant landscape of the serum that has as main features, the predominance of the plateau, the clouds of all the colors, the blue sky and the dry and pure air. Although they already know the place, they can't stop wondering about the spectacle of nature.

However, despite all this beauty, the concern for the future was great on everyone's side. After all, a whole job was at stake and depending on the outcome of this endeavor, peace, and justice could reign in a time of great social inequality, lack of most, dry from time to time, and a complete political structure, completely twisted political structure.

Everything was about to happen; Angel's group finally visualizes the farm. At the chief's signal, everyone goes down and continues the rest of the walk. They walk with steady, safe and determined steps towards the entrance of the imposing farm headquarters that was well guarded. Any moment now, they would be detected.

That's what doesn't take long. As they penetrate others territory, the contention begins with each one choosing their opponent.

The following groups of battle are formed, Angel versus Esmeralda, Victor versus Clementina, Marcela versus Patricia, Penelope versus Helius, Rafael versus Henry and Cangaceiros versus Romeo. In the most 30 minutes, we'd have to have some positive results for one side.

The battle begins intense. The vision concentrates on the efforts of those involved revealing me the following: Angel uses his experience with white magic versus the black magic of the rival. Usually, the contest is balanced. Well, with the advantage and the fall of the other. In the hardest times, each of which is worth their symbols and personal faith, Angel, with his crucifix and Esmeralda with the Pentagon, between Victor and Clementina, there is a slight advantage to the first for the fact that he is immune to his personal faith, where he is the powers of the second. However, he has to keep his attention wide open

Bloody Battle

because any carelessness can be deadly in front of this dangerous opponent, in the dispute of the Fire Lord Patricia takes advantage by moving quickly in space-time leaving Marcela helpless in every moment. Finally, the cangaceiros meet at a screaming disadvantage despite their efforts in front of the heavyweight Romeo.

The score was 2×2. Even as time goes by, the situation doesn't change to the point of any team taking advantage over the other decisively. The time stipulated for the fight began to fade.

Coming up close to the end, Angel for one reason or another, gets distracted, and the opponent takes the opportunity to hurt him, leaving him unconscious. This fact affects everyone in individual fights, especially Victor who even with his prejudices, loved him discreetly. With the lion's strength, you rule out your opponent, approaching Esmeralda. Your other companions start to lose by nervous.

Before the complete approach, the spirits that accompany him inform him that a great decision has to be made. Otherwise, a curse was about to be released by rebooting an ancient confrontation that nearly destroyed the universe.

Far away, spiritual figures are invoked by Esmeralda. Shadows and light have prepared to confront once again with their leaders Miguel and Lucifer. However, there was still a chance to avoid this tragedy, and it was in the hands of the mighty young Victor.

Following his intuition and all he learned from his masters of life, Victor asked the benign forces of the universe what attitude to take and the answer he received was the word "delivery."

Immediately, his eyes opened to reality and realized the only way out of it, a very painful one. However, if I didn't try, many lives and dreams would be lost. He couldn't leave everyone nearly darkness.

In a heroic attitude, he took his crucifix, he threw it towards the opponent and said, "I do!" Immediately, the curse was broken, the tranquility returned, the evil mutants lost their strength, falling disgracefully. Victory to the side of good began to consolidate.

He still had time to approach his fallen master, touch him and say,

"I love you!

Everyone hears it. After he took seven steps ahead and fell down. There was the saga of that young battler, the legendary family of psychics, the Torres.

After the fact, Esmeralda and her group withdrew defeated and powerless. Angel's group met next to the dead. They found themselves distressed by one more loss. First Ramon, now Victor, blood spilled for freedom.

A few minutes later, Angel got up recovered. When he heard the sad news, he convulsively cried next to his wife. They respected each other even though they loved the same person.

Overcome the initial shock, the group withdrew the body of Victor for a decent burial. But the saga still wasn't finished.

2.85-Return

The funeral was held within normal with the presence of families, families, relatives, and friends. At the end, an urgent meeting was organized with some leadership and revolting. In common agreement, they decided to organize a march towards the Carabais farm headquarters to demand their rights.

Gathering a crowd about 500 people, the march moved from the village to the headquarters of the Carabais farm. They'll complete the course in about 15 minutes. At the gate, they were answered by the colonel's servants who referred the order to the same.

A few moments later, they were informed that he would only meet the leaders of the riot. Then they were selected three people who together would fight for everyone's right.

The three representatives had access to the main headquarters, accompanied by the servants, who led them to a private room in the big house. Inside, locked doors, began to debate about the claims of the general population exposing their views.

Feeling backed up and without support, the colonel gave in to the pressure granting most claims. The representatives have been pleased with the result of your demonstration. Of course, there would be for a long time, remnants of prejudice, corruption, of injustices and fates coronelism.

But the important thing was that it had been taken the first step. Most of it was on the responsibility of the groups of vigilantes, heroes of aggress and serpent. Among them, the founders Angel and the Torres brothers stood out They were young battlers and warriors who had somehow marked their name in history. The last two besides leaving their example of life had honored their last name and perpetuated themselves as in the case of Victor who had made Penelope pregnant.

The Torres' psychic line would continue in generation and generation. Death wasn't the end. It was just a start of a new trajectory. In this first cycle, the encounter between two worlds, it involves love, passion, fights, and action.

1- *Wake up*

Co-vision's gone. Slowly, Renato and I will resume consciousness. Everything we'd lived through was nothing but a time-lapse revealing of mysteries that had not lasted more than 30 minutes.

After waking up, we greet each other moved by the beautiful story revealed. Would we have the same disposition and courage as the legendary Victor? Of course, the situations were totally different. We were young of the 21st century, an early age of his more than his even with many challenges to fulfill.

Basically, if we could follow your example, surely victories would happen more easily. However, reiterating, the situations were incomparable.

At a quick meeting, we decided to return to the master's house. This would be a good opportunity to expand our knowledge and ask for a safer guidance regarding how to continue.

Certainly, we advance, facing the same difficulties as ever, worlds with positive and motivating thought over the future of our venture. Now all I had left was to move on with my head held high.

The full course was carried out in approximately half an hour at regular and steady steps. We're finally here. In front of the hovel, we stopped a little at this point, we were thrilled because we were about to find out what fate was reserving us or at least a forwarding which would be key to our double.

Instants later, we partially overcome our entrances. Once we realized the door was unlocked, we walked in without asking for permission because we already considered ourselves home.

We found the master. He was in the middle of the house, with his eyes closed to meditate. A little afraid, we approach him and touch him with the purpose of waking him up. Then he opens his eyes, sketches a smile and gets up. With a sign, he asks us to sit down and start a conversation.

"Well? Did it work out with the co-vision technique?"

"It was wonderful. In a matter of seconds, a film was passed on in our minds. Very interesting indeed. It was worth it! (The psychic)

"What now? What's the next step? (Renato)

"Step two. Inspiring in history revealed, you must also seek to achieve the great miracle: "The meeting of two worlds." This will only be possible if there's too much dedication on your part. (Angel)

"How's that going? (The psychic)

"The key to the question is in training. Find the healer in Carabais. He still lives in the Painted Place. In your experience, you must know the best way to reach the goal. My share is already fulfilled, and it was a success. Now I can rest in peace. It was nice meeting you. Aldivan and Renato, success on their walk. Keep it up all the time. You will still be proud of this state and country.

"Thank you for everything, master. We'll never forget him. (The psychic)

"We'll take your lessons forward. For right and fair! (Renato)

Bloody Battle

"All for one and all for one! (Angel)

"For the humble and wronged! Friends forever! (The psychic)

The emotion has taken over the moment. We're up. As we approach each other, our action resulted in a triple hug. For a moment, we feel the strength of our feelings, friendship. With our union, a small torch of fire came down from the sky, lighting the whole place. There, there was our star guide, who would help us in the hardest times.

When the embrace ended, the torch went back to the place of origin. We're done saying goodbye. With tears in our eyes, we finally retreat from our benefactor. We've crossed the door. On the outside, we begin the walk to the village of Cimbres. A new stage in sight and that promised many emotions and discoveries. Keep following, readers.

From the beginning of the new journey, we kept at the disposal, claw, and courage from always similar to the first challenge than the mountain. Although they were different situations, the feeling was the same. Besides, precaution, patience, and tranquility were also cultivated because they were fundamental to a possible success. Lesson learned during the road of life with the convivial with excellent masters. That included friends, family, spiritual advisors.

Everything could work out or not. The most important thing was learning and evolution achieved with every new experience. We become eternal apprentices. To achieve that, we would continue to move on with our heads held high, growing values like dignity, friendship, simplicity, loyalty, and transparency. This was the brand of the dynamic duo of the series the psychic formed by the psychic and young Renato.

The saga continued. We're going through places we've known; we're pleased to relive various situations. Our imagination is in the line of time and space. How many feet had not passed through their full of expectations? To stand out from the crowd, we needed an intense dedication to our projects. Something we didn't need, thank God.

Created as always in our cause and inspiring us in our ancestors, we increase the pace of steps. A few minutes later, we've already spotted the famous Cimbres houses. At this point, we thought unreliable efforts forts that were unreliable. But we were hoping it would work out.

With 500 more meters down, we finally have access to the main street. When we get to the Church of Our Lady of the Mountains, a self-filled pass. We give her signal and she stops. We're on board. As you had enough passengers, the departure for research is immediate.

All the way through, we have a chance to have a nice chat with the travel companions and with the driver named Balthazar who was very nice. We've talked a bit of everything including general news, sports, music, religion, politics, and relationship in the total of 30 minutes' journey.

At the end of the race, we go down, say goodbye and pay for the ticket. We're waiting for another bus to leave with Arcoverde. We'd be halfway, in the old Carabais, in the purpose of meeting a famous master of the past. He was the healer who was over a hundred years old. What would happen?

Thirty minutes later, five more passengers arrive and then the car finally leaves. This one made; we grow silence. We've enjoyed meditating a little and enjoying nature. Between stops, we spend another 30 minutes on the road.

The car stops at the edge of BR 232, we go down and pay for the ticket. We had a mile of miles on our way to walk to the center of the village. Apart from the route to the painted site we didn't know for sure because we didn't know him yet.

We're starting the new walk. The curves climb made me remember a past not too far away and how nice it felt to taste. I share my memories with Renato, who listens closely and opinions.

Though I was a wise man, and he gives me valuable and secret tips. I also enjoy complimenting the disposition of helping me since you met me. Over time, we had become brothers-friends, accomplices and faithful journey mates. This was key to the success of our endeavor.

Bloody Battle

We're moving on. Completing exactly twenty-five minutes of the climb, we have access to the first houses. When we found the first person, we asked for information on the painted site and the healer's person.

It's about a young blonde, average height, pink faces, called Jaqueline. Describe in detail how to get there. Since you were unoccupied, you offer your company.

We'll take it. We crossed the whole village and took a dirt road. Right at first, we make conversation with the girl with the intent to get to know each other better and spend a little time.

"What are you doing for the bands, Miss? (The psychic)

"I work as a health agent for three days a week. In my spare time, I do housework. In my house, there are four people, me, my sister and my parents. And you? (Jaqueline)

"I'm a public servant and in the spare hours, a beginner writer. I work on my projects with my assistant Renato. (The psychic)

"This. I'm a key piece in stories. (Declared proud Renato)

"Very well. What kind of writing? (Jaqueline)

"Realistic fiction. But I wish to write real stories too. Did you get any tips? (The psychic)

"No. I only know simple people. But trust God will provide. (Jaqueline)

"I believe you too. (Renato)

"So be it. Maktub! (The psychic)

"By putting the books aside, is it still far from the healer's house? (Renato)

"Not much. Why? (Jaqueline)

"I'm hungry. (Renato)

"Calm down. Let's keep walking quietly. You can make yourself comfortable, okay, Jaqueline? (The psychic)

"Thank you.

The conversation instantly stopped. We diverted right into the road and entered a beat verdict facing the dry floor, thorns, and branches of the nearby bushes. But since we were from the place we were used to.

Further ahead, the path spreads a little, and we're more comfortable. In the field of vision, a hovel comes. At the signal of Jaqueline, we're moving forward to him. In about five minutes, we've met at the door about to knock. However, before we did that, the door opens mysteriously. Inside, the figure of the elder, who despite age keeps strong and strong features beyond the peculiar way to dress, leather pants, hat, lace shirt and sole sandals.

With one gesture, he starts the conversation:

"Jack, what are you doing here? What about these others? They look familiar.

"Hi. These are my friends: Seer and Renato. They want to talk to you. (Jaqueline)

"I'm the grandson of Victor. (The psychic)

"And I'm your assistant. (Renato)

"How? I thought so. You look a lot like your grandfather. Welcome. (Healer)

"Thank you. I'm proud of it. Can we come in? (The psychic)

"Yeah, sure. You want to come too, Jack? (Healer)

"No, I'm coming. I just came to accompany you. Even for everyone. (Jaqueline)

"See you.

We're in the house. Accompanying the host, we settle in drums willing in circles at the center of the hovel. After initial silence, the conversation is finally resumed.

"Well, what brought you here, to this end of the world? (Healer)

"We came from an unequal adventure and our master told us to look for him. (The psychic)

"He's called Angel and said that with his help we can achieve the miracle which consume at the meeting between two worlds. Is it really possible? (Renato)

Bloody Battle

The healer's face got stiffed. He stayed for a few static moments to think. In these moments we wished to be powerful telepaths to guess exactly what was going on in your mind.

Since we weren't, we were silent to wait for your statement what happened right after.

Anything is possible, my dear, to depend on the dedication. First, though, I wish to meet you a little more. (Healer)

"Okay. My name is Aldivan Teixeira, also known as the psychic or the son of God. I'm a public official and a writer on the off hours. I come from two incredible adventures along with my assistant Renato who have rented my first two titles: "Opposing Forces" "And the dark night of the soul" I'm on a third project and to get it done, I need your help. (The psychic)

"This. Like he said, I'm your friend and assistant. (Renato)

"Got it. I believe I can help you with your goals. Do you accept training? (Healer)

"Sure. Always. (The psychic)

"We're ready. (Renato complement)

"Very well. For us to achieve success, you must remain here for seven days. As for the accommodations, don't worry. I have enough beds. (Healer)

"Thank you. Is that really necessary? (The psychic)

"Yes. Put your shyness aside and be my guest. Your grandfather wasn't like that. (In laughter, the healer)

"I don't think he's got a way. (Renato)

"Well, I'm going to sleep now. If you're hungry, you can go to the kitchen and prepare something. Training starts tomorrow. (Healer)

"Copy that. (The psychic)

"You can be my guest, master. (Renato)

The healer stood up, stretched and tiresome came near one of the beds. He lay down and immediately fell asleep. Renato and I settled in, we exchanged ideas, and as predicted, we're hungry.

We go to the kitchen and make a quick snack. Thereafter, we left the hovel on a walk around. Three hours later, we came back, and we found the awake master. We talked a little more and offered to help with housework. When we're done, we've performed other study and leisure activities.

With the arrival of the night, we had dinner and went out a little to contemplate the stars. With your experience, the healer gives us some astronomy lessons besides telling some interesting stories of his past.

We've been in this exercise for three hours. When it gets a little late, the healer retires. Since we had nothing to do, we followed him. The other day would be the beginning of a new journey, headed towards the unknown. What fate would reveal itself before us? Were we prepared for what came? These and other unanswered questions were about to be solved. Let's continue the saga of number three.

Two-Fear of God

It's dawn. The sun rises, the birds sing and a soft breeze overcomes the wall flooding the whole environment. In a few moments, we wake up, we crawl, we'll take a shower. In the end, we went to the kitchen and along with the host we prepared breakfast with what we had available in the pantry.

We've taken the opportunity to narrow our ties until recent. When the food is ready, we sit at the table, and we serve ourselves in a communion ritual.

We feed in silence and respect. When we're done, we start a conversation to direct doubts.

"When do we start our training? (The psychic)

"In a minute. First, I want to know how Angel trained them. (Healer)

"I'll explain. We passed the test of development of the Holy Spirit gifts. It was six steps total with them, we could develop a new technique, the co-vision that provided us with the first step vision. (Renato)

Bloody Battle

"I see. We must then continue on this line of reasoning until it reaches the top of the second stage. What was the gift left? (Healer)

"It was the fear of God. (The psychic)

"We'll start from there. Follow me. (Healer)

We obey the master by heading out. We've overstepped all obstacles. Out of the way, we move on by walking a verdict in the same way. Ten minutes later, walking vigorously, we entered a clearing. At the master's signal, we sat in the center of it from then on, he starts explaining.

I brought you here for a healthy debate. A trade of experiences because there's no one in this world so wise that can't learn or anyone so ignorant that they can't teach. Everyone, very or very, has luggage. (Healer)

"I agree. Life is characterized by a continuous teaching process, a very used term in education. (The psychic)

"Says the teacher! But tell us, master, what have you to tell us about the gift of God\8 (Renato)

"From experience, unlike most people think, God doesn't want us to be afraid of him. It requires respect, dedication to its cause, following its laws and practical works in exchange for your love and protection. "However, even those who insist on their mistakes, who are sunk in their darkened night², are not abandoned by the divine. This happens because he, above all, is a father and is good to everyone. This consists of perfection. What about you? What concept do you have of this gift? (Healer)

"Look, master, in the period I was immersed in my dark night of my soul, I could have the dimension of two opposites of God, mercy and justice. At that time, I was totally carried away by my messenger, coming to think I owned the world. That's when the forces of good acted and imposed me their strength. They opened my eyes, punished me, and then I realized the evil I had done. However, despite the insistent requests of my enemies, instead of convicting me, God freed me and resurrected not just this time, but countless times. God is a father.

The only condition that imposes us is a commitment to not repeating the same mistakes. In short, for all I've lived, I can conclude that we must grow the fear of God. We must not light your wrath because your hand is too heavy for us mortals and fair. Beyond justice, there is mercy. This is only achieved if we earn your trust. We must have attitude and position. (I, the psychic)

"Despite my little age, I have something to tell you too. Ever since my mother passed away, my father treated me hard. From him, I learned from fear and fear never dictated my actions. This was my experience of a human father. When I ran away, I found the mountain guardian and with her, I had a more dignified life. I could study, have friends, play and work, too. I found out with her teachings and investigating in books, a real father. A father who doesn't strike, who loves, who accepts us as we are, a truly human father. The fear, to me, is a father-son relationship. Like any relationship, you need debate, knowledge, complicity, fidelity, and loyalty. It's the only way it becomes complete. But we must never be afraid. It keeps us from God. (Renato)

"Splendid! Different opinions, but all meaningful. I've noticed the strong influence of personal experiences in your opinions. This is normal. I think we can try. (Healer)

"Try what? (The psychic)

"I have the same doubt too. (Renato)

"Complete the first cycle, the seven gifts. With proper lighting, we can absorb knowledge and make sure that way to continue to achieve a complete goal. (Healer)

"Okay. We can try. (The psychic)

"How do we act? (Renato)

"Get up and form a circle. (Healer)

We obey the master. We hold hands and close the circle. Immediately, he kneels, prays shortly and asks us to go through the past challenges. In a matter of seconds, we reminisce the most remarkable moments of adventure to the present moment. Prayer finished, the

Bloody Battle

master rises, and raises with ours, hands to heaven. Suddenly, the world trembles, darkens, and tongues like fire come down on our heads.

From there, we enter complete ecstasy. We are filled with the power from above similar to what happened to the apostles of Christ. That's about two thousand years ago.

This wonderful moment lasts only 30 seconds. When the fire languages are finished, we meet again just the three of us. The master then takes the word.

"I got it. I know the way to go. Shall we? (Healer)

"Could you give us a head start? (The psychic)

"No. Every day your concern. Let's go home. (Healer)

"Okay. Shall we, Renato? (The psychic)

"Sure. (Renato)

Our trio began to go back and the questions kept coming into our minds. What would happen? Whatever it was we believed we were ready to face it because we had experience in challenges.

For now, the master was right, there was nothing to worry about. The first step had already been taken. Now all I had left was to move on with race, courage, without fear and shameless to be happy.

With a little dedication and luck, we could get to the desired results. But this was the future.

While this one didn't arrive, we kept walking. About the same time as the trip, we arrived at the hovel. During the rest of the day, we'd be involved in other activities that had nothing to do with the challenge.

At night, we'd learn more about the universe and trade experiences. The master would plan the next steps and live the expectation of the next day that promised many new things.

When we were tired, we'd rest. It was usually early because in the place there weren't many entertainment options.

Keep following, readers.

3- *The value of friendship*

Night usually works. The dawn passes and dawn then. At the first light of the sun, we awaken. Immediately each of you will occupy in an activity the master will prepare breakfast while me and my faithful fellow adventures will take a bath.

In 30 minutes, we fulfill the obligation. We went to the room and changed our clothes. All right, let's go to the kitchen. Once we get there, we serve ourselves and the master takes advantage of himself.

Meanwhile, Renato and I exchanged classified information. But we don't have much time for this because in less than ten minutes the master will return. He sits with us at the table and politely waits for us to break up, so he can pronounce himself what doesn't take long.

"Did you sleep well? (Healer)

"Except for some nightmares, all right. (Inform Renato)

"Normal Just a little anxious. (Confessed, the psychic)

"Very well. Then let's get started. With the lighting I had yesterday, I thought it'd be best to continue the training of the same way I started. A conversation with total freedom, respect, and interaction. Agreed? (Healer)

"No problem. (The psychic)

"That's an interesting method. What are we going to talk about? (I wanted to know Renato)

"Today's theme is friendship. It contains a little of your trajectory and experience in this sense. (Healer)

"I'll start. Friendship to me is everything. I learned this from the higher spirits, my family, friends, acquaintances, coworkers, spiritual masters and life. On this path, I loved, I suffered, I cried, I missed, I hit, I fought, and I got confused. But I got over it and forgave it. Anyway, I learned, I thought, and I want to keep moving on after all. (The psychic)

"My beginning of history, as you know, is a little tragic. I only knew the good feelings when I met the guardian. She's my benefactor. That's

Bloody Battle

when I had a greater contact with society. In them, there are schoolmates and my dear fellow adventure. (Renato)

"Thank you. (The psychic)

"What would you do for a needy friend? (Healer)

"Depends. If he was confused, I'd advise him. If you were in trouble, we'd try to find a solution together. In short, I'd help whatever was necessary. (The psychic)

"I'd put myself at my disposal at good times and bad times. (Explained Renato summarily)

"I like it. It would help, too. In this world, we're all the same. What we bring with concrete is good deeds. Money, pride, vanity, sorrows, disputes and selfishness lead to nothing. However, it is still very common to hear from false friends when you need the following sentence: "Not my problem." (Healer)

"Exactly. It's happened to me a lot. But I'm not like them. I'm not going to repeat that mistake. (The psychic)

"Good. Even without much experience, I've seen cases of people who revolted and started acting the same way. (Renato comment)

"Don't ever do that. Even if the blood boils, don't mix with this kind of people. We need to get values and not share. (Healer)

"Jesus is the example. (The psychic)

"He's the main one. They are also remarkable Mother Teresa of Calcutta, Sister Dulce, Zilda Arns, Dorothy Stang, Mother Paulina, Francisco Xavier of Cassia, Santa Rita of Cassia, Nelson Mandela, Francis of Assisi, among thousands of examples. (Healer)

"I've heard of it. They were spectacular. (Renato)

"Is it possible to get to their level of evolution, master? (The psychic)

"Don't compare yourself to anyone. Each has its peculiar history. The important thing is to grow good values, have experiences that life provides, have good companies, live and not be ashamed of being happy as music says. Time teaches. (Healer)

"Got it. I'll move on then. (The psychic)

With my help, we can keep scoring history and charming hearts in the serial psychic. (Renato)

"This. Follow fate with claw, strength, and faith that success will come as a consequence. Don't forget about me and the others. That's what friendship is. (Healer)

"Of course not. We value our origins. (I, the psychic)

"How about a hug? (Renato)

The emotion took over us all, and we accepted young Renato's suggestion. We're up. When you get close, the triple hug happens to last a few moments. There was a trio battling, seeking knowledge. Though they belonged to different worlds, they were united by fate. Every step of the way, the revealing meeting was approaching.

Finished the hug, we walked away. The master says goodbye, explaining he had chores to do in the village. When you leave, it's just the two of us. We have the idea to fix the hovel. Although it wasn't much of our beach, only good intention was valid.

When the master returned, we would continue to help him in other activities until the day are over. One more step has been accomplished. With the healer's experience, great lessons had stayed. Let's move on.

4-*complicity.*

A new day comes with the usual features. At some point, a cold wind hits our bodies already recovered from the previous efforts causing us to wake up. Immediately, I gather enough courage and strength to lift. I try one, two, three, four times. I'll catch up with the success last time.

Furthermore, in addition, I watch my helper closely. I see that despite awake, my fellow adventure has not yet been disposed of at least effort. So, I decide to approach and fondly help you take an initiative. Five minutes later, both are already standing up.

In a quick conversation, we share the chores, and we'll be done. This one made, Renato and I prepared breakfast by exercising our cooking gifts. Meanwhile, the master takes his bath quickly. When you finish this task, change your clothes and meet us still in the kitchen.

When it comes to the environment, it still gives him time to suggest some improvements on the plate that at the time it's made of couscous with a bubbly cooked macaroon. We appreciate the help, and we'll give the final touch on the meal.

With everything ready, we serve ourselves and sit at the table. While we eat, we start a friendly conversation.

First, I want to thank you for all your attention and dedication to our cause. But I still have some doubts left. Could you sanction them? (The psychic)

"Depends. You'll get all the answers you need in time. The nerves and anxiety are just in the way. (Healer)

"It's nothing extraordinary. I want to know how many stages we have to perform and how to achieve the most desired miracle. (The psychic)

"Like I said, it's going to be seven days of training. In this period, I request full focus on your part. The rest will come as a consequence. (Healer)

"Okay. I'll wait. Any questions, Renato? (The psychic)

"Besides yours, I'm curious to know the true name of our worthy master. (Renato)

"You're asking too much. My baptism name is Secret. For now, stick to training and not silly things. (SCREAMS THE MASTER)

"Okay. Sorry for the nerve. (Renato)

"Don't worry. Finish feeding. (Healer)

The master's voice sounded serious and firm. That makes us disciples take the request as order. Quietly, we continue to taste food very slowly. We ate a portion of each and since we were still feeling hungry, we repeat the dose.

Twelve minutes later, we're finally satisfied. When we're finished, we head to the improvised bathroom to take care of our body. One at a time. Between bathing, change clothes and back to the kitchen we spent more forty minutes of our precious time.

However, despite the delay, we find the radiant master and once again willing to help us.

"Can we get started? (Healer)

"Yes. (Me and Renato)

"Well, the subject approached today is complicity. Could you share your experiences in that sense? (Healer)

"Sure. I can say, undoubtedly, that this is one of my principal features. In any relationship it's significant. For example, in difficulties, we seek support. We're looking for someone to trust and share the weight of responsibilities. In case we don't find it, life gets a little emptier and sadder. Complicity and trust are two important links. (The psychic)

"I agree. We should also be as careful as we can to deposit our trust in the right people. (Renato)

"Excellent, Renato. But it's hard at first to have this ability of judgment. Precaution must be the key word and knowledge is something necessary. Only with him is possible to decide. (Alerted the master)

"Have you ever had disappointments, master? (Renato)

"Lots. It's part of the process of evolution. The important thing is not to repeat the same mistakes. (Healer)

"Good point. I've also lived something similar over and over again. Mistakes make the way to the right. (I've been pushing)

Exactly, my dear. Congratulations. I believe you will soon harvest the fruits of your work. They always persist. (Healer)

"Got it. Thanks again. (Renato)

"You're welcome. Shall we take care of the house? (Healer)

"Yes. (Both of us)

We'll take the necessary material and start the suggested activity. When we're done, we'd do other pertinent jobs. The most important thing was that we're progressing in sight. Heading to success!

Five-reflections.

The other day, we performed the morning's correctional activities as usual and as we finished eating breakfast we met at the center of the hovel by the master's nomination. We sit on the floor next to each other. After a moment, finally the healer takes the initiative.

"Well, we're here again on the fifth day of training. Are you enjoying it so far? (Healer)

"Yeah. But I must confess that I expected something more spectacular with incredible techniques, mysteries to be solved and extraordinary revelations. (The psychic)

"It's been a great learning apprentice for me. I have nothing to complain about. (Renato)

"Got it. Seer, it's normal for someone like you, with a great experience in adventure to expect this concept. But believe me, we'll have more concrete results acting this way. We need to do the information exchange. As for you, Renato, feel free. (The master)

"Thank you. (Renato)

"What's the next move? (The psychic)

"We'll talk about a complex and universal theme today, love. What are your opinions? (Healer)

"As for love, I've tried everything. I felt the spiritual love of God, of delivery and complete resignation. Besides, I felt human love. It's something that involves attraction, approach, faith and convicted strength. However, regarding this last one, my experiences were not good. (The psychic)

"For my little age, I have experienced family love and passion is not too deep. As you know, my life has not been easy. (Renato)

"We understand Renato and admire him. In time, you'll have a chance to know true love. As for you, psychic, not discouragement. Happiness will come to you in the right time. The most important thing is to persevere in the fight to be happy because that's actually what matters. (Advised the healer)

"I hope so. And you? What are your experiences regarding love? (The psychic)

"Well, like any human being who's lived over a hundred years, I know a little of life. However, my spiritual work and the relationship with nature have always come in the first place. In a way, it kept me from people. That's it. We live on choices and mine were well thought. I don't regret it. (Healer)

"I agree. Making choices is the main act to become the main actors on the stage of our lives. Being a leader of yourself is the main goal. (The psychic)

"And the consequences come! (Renato complement)

"That's exactly what I want to pass to your disciples. I wish from the bottom of my heart that they have the courage and strength to make their decisions and face them without fear of contradicting the greatest who support a false moral in our society. Be like the legendary Victor and his group of vigilantes who have marked history at an even harder time than the present. (Healer)

"We promised to try this way. (The psychic)

Together, we can get the miracle, the so-awaited meeting between two worlds and hearts. (Declared with optimism, Renato)

"That's the way to talk. I like to see it. Any more observations? (Healer)

"No. What about you, Renato? (The psychic)

"Neither. (Renato)

"Very well. Today's work is over here. I'm going out for a while, visiting some friends in the village. You guys take care of home and think about our conversation. (Healer)

"Okay. See you. (The psychic)

"See you. (Renato)

"Hug. See you in a bit. (Healer)

That said, the master walked away, opened the door and left. Now it was just me and Renato. We would follow the master's advice and when he returned, he would be proud of us because dedication and commitment would not miss our part. Let's continue our saga then.

6-Mediunity.

One more day has passed. After we got up, tighten up, shower, eat breakfast and brush our teeth, we reunited with the healer. This one made, we settled in the bed located in his room. After locking the doors, the master had the safety needed to start the conversation.

"Well, ready?

"We always are. (The psychic)

"I believe so. (Renato)

"I thought about it. I've come to the conclusion that you make necessary at this time, the use of two techniques. Today, I'll teach you the first ones. It's about the improvement of medium. (Inform the healer)

"Very nice. Despite the various experiences I've had, I'm not fully developed. (Confessed, the psychic)

"Interesting. I have no experience. But in my case, is it possible? Even though, I don't have a specific gift. (Renato)

"Answering to both of you, you're never fully prepared. We're all high-level psychics. The question is how to prepare properly for these beyond life contacts that often save us from great dangers. I have one of the keys to reach this. (Healer)

"We're all ears. (I've prepared)

"Go ahead, master. (Ratified Renato)

"We've been living for six days, and I've realized your ability and value. Above all, they have given me confidence, and therefore I will reveal one of my secrets. Listen up. (Healer)

The master stood up and approached the walls. Specifically, from one of the paintings nailed with excellent taste. He took it out, leaving the show a mirror, the one we had visualized in the history of Victor.

With a signal, he asks for our approach. Once we get close, he'll come back to us.

Close your eyes and concentrate on infinity. With this in mind, just once in the mirror.

We obey once more. When we feel prepared, we play simultaneously the mirror. Immediately, we enter into a kind of transcend our spirits overcome the various existing dimensions, we pass through the heavens, hell, the city of men, purgatory, limbo, the abyss, dimensional doors, planets of the entire universe.

The experience is perfect and fast. Forty seconds, we're back on consciousness. When we woke up, we left the mirror. We're back to sitting while the master next to us seems anxious and restless. Let's start the dialogue again.

"That's wonderful! I've never felt so light and loose. It's like my senses are at the bottom of my skin, without any communication barrier. (He observed)

"I felt something like that, too. Although they are a different world than ours, this technique shows how possible the encounter is, even though it's so desperate realities. (Renato)

"Glad you understood. As long as they have access to the second technique, they can complement this one, they will have the opportunity to achieve the miracle they so desire. It will be the right time for a reevaluation of life giving the opportunity to stipulate new goals and consolidate the already achieved. Anyway, a new walk that will be long if God wants. (Healer)

"That's great! Let's get on with the work, shall we, Renato? (The Son of God)

"Sure. But now I'm hungry. Can we prepare something? (Renato)

Renato's naivety provoked laughter at me and the master. What a character! Without him, the series the psychic wouldn't have the same charm he has.

When we control ourselves, we start talking again.

"Okay. Shall we go, master? (The psychic)

"Be my guest. For today, no more training. But don't forget to clean up the mess. (Healer)

"Okay. (The psychic and Renato)

Right away, we get up from the bed. We took a few steps, we opened the door and moved towards the kitchen. Once we got there, we started making a scramble of rice and beans seasoned with what we had available. In ten minutes, we'll finish prepping. Even though I'm not hungry, I'm following Renato into the tasting of this delight which I specialize in.

During the feeding, we share experiences and expectations. What was expecting us from now on? Would our effort be rewarded? What good would we take from this adventure for the rest of our lives? These and other questions would soon be answered in such a desired meeting.

While the time was not right, we'd be able to refuel. At the end, we begin other everyday activities. Forward, forever! For readers and the universe so unique that it provided gifts! Forward!

7-O secret to the seven doors.

The seventh day of experiences and internal fights carried out in the cottage of the mysterious healer Early, we rise at a frenetic rhythm and perform the usual activities in a record time.

I'm done with breakfast; I don't contain my nerves and anxiety. Start, because the conversation with the others.

"What now, master? Could you guide us in definitive? (The psychic)

"Already? Are you really ready? (Healer)

"I believe so, what about you, Renato? (The Son of God)

"I'm with you, my friend. Let's move on. (Renato)

"Brave of you. You know, but what are you going to face? (Healer)

"No. But it doesn't matter much. What's life worth without adventures or meaningless? In my opinion, a total void. (The psychic)

"Explain to us better master. (Renato requested)

"I like it. The next challenge is a big secret I've never revealed to anyone. Only if they do, they'll have a chance of achieving the wished miracle. You guys up for it? (Healer)

"What exactly is this about? (Renato)

"I usually call it a secret of the seven doors. It's several overlapped dimensions and every minute the situation gets even more complicated. If they fail, they can be trapped in one of their parallel dimensions. What do you say? (Healer)

"Excuse me, Renato, as leader of this venture, I decide you'll stay out of this stage. Don't get me wrong, it's just that I have a greater experience in extreme situations. I'd rather continue only from now on. All right? (The psychic)

"I don't understand it very well, but I do. (Renato)

What should I do, master? (The psychic)

"First, follow me. (Healer)

I obeyed the master and along with him, we followed to the room. We passed the door and locked it. Once we're absolutely certain of being alone, we'll be communicating again.

"Close your eyes. (Asked the healer)

Even though I thought it was strange, I obeyed again. About 30 seconds later, I hear your voice again and this one's asking me to open them. In doing so, I have a stunning vision of a portal ahead of us and in my eyes of doubt the master is about to pronounce himself.

"Here is the gate of knowledge created by me. I'm one of the few in the land capable of it. He's like an enlarged reality. Open the door, pray to your guardian angel and overtake the obstacles. At the end, you'll find your way out.

"When can I go? (The psychic)

"Immediately. Hurry, because there's a time limit. (Inform the healer)

"Okay. (The Son of God)

I start taking the first steps and even though I fight my fears I keep going on and on. I'll pull over. Furthermore, I'll stop for five seconds and breathe. When I'm done with this time, I'm grabbing the handle, I open the door, I take two steps and I close it behind me. What I see at first makes me impressed.

Bloody Battle

I'm in a flat, dark, extensive, and totally cryptic place. In a moment, the sky and the ground disappear and my body starts floating in the air helped by my secret techniques. I begin then, without definite direction. In time, I'm tired of myself, I'm thinking by asking for assistance from the higher forces that follow me and as an answer, a mysterious voice says that everything is about to begin. Trust that, for a little while and rest, supposed to be in the air. Next thing I know, I hear a ribbon echoing and pairs of lights and powerful shadows coming closer. With the experience, I have of the spirit plan, I realize the presence closer to them, which are the seven spirits of God. But what was the plan that carried them? To what end? Flying at the speed of light, they quickly arrive and surround me completely: are seven angelic warriors of the highest hierarchy, with their pairs of amazing wings, swords, spears, and stars ready for combat. Right away, I try to keep telepathic contact with the same. I'm successful because a conversation begins soon.

"What do you want from me? (I, the psychic)

We're here to prove your faith. To move on, you'll have to beat us in a fight. (Speaking of Miguel, the boss)

"Excuse me? (I asked incredulous)

"That's right human. What you want is beyond the possibility for mortals, and we request from God this proof. (Lucifer, the Black Archangel)

"Got it. But shouldn't you be taking care of the humans? I don't understand the point of this fight. (The psychic)

"We are light and darkness in a total of seven. Together we are the divinity. We decided this because this is a sacred place you dared to penetrate. (All in choir)

"But don't worry. Since you are the son of God, can easily defeat us. (Lucifer laughs)

The other holy ones laughed and their voices looked like thunder riff. What would now be the son of God? He's resolved to answer.

"In the plan I'm just a human. But what you don't know is that I left God in spirit. There were many reincarnations on planet Earth for millennia and finally in this I got contact with the father. Today we are one because God is present in every innocent child, in every devoted mother and father, in orphans, in the poor and wronged of this world. Jesus is the example because he was the first human to have the courage to say that God is a father. Which is a great truth because everyone who follows his law is their children regardless of creed, sexual option, religion or social position. God is the meeting of good hearts and even though it's just a poor human I know it. (I claimed)

"Blasphemy! Finish him. (Incited Lucifer)

My attitude incited the wrath of the archangels, and they're all over me. However, I didn't care. I had disconnected and answered the charge. And that it was what God wanted.

At the moment the swords were ready to hit me in half, a shield protected me and rid me of the attacks. Soon the thunder laughed, filled the environment and the world shivered.

By my side was my spiritual guide. At his signal, everyone knelt down. Immediately, we feel the presence of the living God.

Since we were inferior beings, we couldn't see him just listen to him. What was said was obvious, there would be no battle! Man is the high point of creation and angels only messengers. End of story!

God withdrew partially and the angels have driven away to occupy their righteous places in the realms. Just me and my guardian. Catching me in the lap, he flies fast. Personally, I'll pass through the doors in a total of seven. In the end, the angel leaves me. Unlocking the last door, I have access to a new environment. To my surprise, I'm back in the room, meeting the master.

With a curious face, he resumes the conversation immediately.

"Did it work out, son of God? (Healer)

"Yes. It was really an incredible and unique experience. What now? What's the next step?

"Now the big moment has come. Wait a minute! (Healer)

Bloody Battle

He walked away a little and opened the bedroom door. Shaking his hair, screaming, "Renato, come here!" In a few moments, he answers the call and enters the room. The door is locked again and there's the three of us, the three Musketeers.

The master signals, we hold hands and form a circle. He starts to guide us.

"We're ready to start a great trip that defies the space-time line. First, we must concentrate on our inner self, fixing the thought of an important fact of our life. When we reach the full concentration, we can walk carefully through the past-present future of existence. However, we must be meticulous not to alter the order of the facts.

"Got it. Something like the trip we've made in the past. (CLICKS THE PINTER)

"Can we get started? (Renato)

"Yes. (The healer)

Following the master's guidance, we begin the ritual of time passage. Every moment of this job, we discover a new world inside ourselves. Instantly, our spirits and bodies tremble with emotion that we have access to the line of existence. Without fear, I string back time and my distressed spirit begins to penetrate a whole new world. Here comes the co-vision of the second part.

The end

www.ingramcontent.com/pod-product-compliance
Lightning Source LLC
LaVergne TN
LVHW021049100526
838202LV00079B/5296